Written by
Stephen Rickard

Ransom

This is Woodlands Farm.
It is Farmer Jack's farm.

It is a big farm.

Farmer Jack has lots of cows on his farm.

The cows moo in the corner.

Farmer Jack has ducks on his farm.

The ducks are in the farmyard.

Quack! Quack! Quack!
The ducks sit in the mud.

They are deep in mud.

Will Farmer Jack keep zebras
on his farm?

No!

Will Farmer Jack keep pandas
on his farm?

No!

Will Farmer Jack keep camels
on his farm? No!

Zebras, pandas and camels are not
for keeping on a farm.

Farmer Jack has a dog on his farm.

This is Spot. He is Farmer Jack's dog.

Spot barks and wags his tail.
He waits for Farmer Jack.

Now the sun is setting.
Spot needs his bed.

Farmer Jack needs his bed too.
Looking after cows is a hard job.

Farmer Jack and Spot go indoors.
Farmer Jack will sleep well tonight.

Good night, Farmer Jack.
Good night, Spot.